ALL ACTION
BACK PACKING

JIMMY HOLMES

LERNER PUBLICATIONS COMPANY
MINNEAPOLIS

Titles in this series
Backpacking
Canoeing
Climbing
Mountain Biking
Skateboarding
Skiing
Survival Skills
Wind and Surf

Photographs are reproduced by permission of: pp. 38, 39, 42, 43, Eye Ubiquitous; cover (front and back), pp. 5, 7, 9, 11, 13 (both), 14, 18, 22, 23, 24, 25, 27, 28, 29, 30, 31, 32 (both), 33, 34, 35, 36, 37, 40, 44, 45 (top), Jimmy Holmes; p. 8, The Hutchison Library; pp. 4, 10, 12, 16, 17, 19 (both), 21 (both), 26, 45 (bottom), Mountin' Excitement; p. 41, U.S. Geological Survey; and p. 6, Zefa.

First published in the United States in 1992
by Lerner Publications Company

All U.S. rights reserved. No part of this book may be reproduced or transmitted in any form or by any means, electronic or mechanical, including photocopying and recording, or by any information storage or retrieval system, without permission in writing from the publisher, except for the inclusion of brief quotations in an acknowledged review.

© Copyright 1991 Wayland (Publishers) Limited
First published in 1991 by Wayland (Publishers) Ltd
61 Western Rd, Hove, East Sussex BN3 1JD, England

Library of Congress Cataloging-in-Publication Data
Holmes, Jimmy.
    Backpacking / Jimmy Holmes.
      p. cm. — (All action)
    Includes index.
    Summary: An introduction to backpacking, discussing equipment and clothing, planning and training for trips, map reading, and proper handling of dangerous situations.
    ISBN 0-8225-2479-1
    1. Backpacking—Juvenile literature. [1. Backpacking.]
I. Title. II. Series.
GV199.6.H65 1992
796.5'1—dc20   91-28021
                                                                   CIP
                                                                     AC

Printed in Italy
Bound in the United States of America
1 2 3 4 5 6 7 8 9 10 01 00 99 98 97 96 95 94 93 92

Contents

STEPPING OUT 4

GETTING STARTED 10

EQUIPMENT 18

HIT THE ROAD 22

HIGH ADVENTURE 28

TOUGHEN UP 38

WHERE AM I? 40

SURVIVAL SKILLS 44

GLOSSARY 46

BOOKS AND VIDEOS 47

MORE INFORMATION 48

INDEX 48

STEPPING OUT

We spend most of our lives in some kind of building — at school, college, work, or home. Often this cozy world is centrally heated or cooled. We can easily sit indoors all day, entertaining ourselves with video games, radio, television, and videos. It's easy to forget what it is like outside in the elements. By gathering some equipment, you can find a whole new world outside your door. Leave behind your television screen and your stuffy indoor life and go backpacking, camping, hiking, or trekking — whatever you want to call it.

There's nothing like being out in the wind and sun — or even in the rain and snow. If you are dressed right, even a walk in the rain can be a lot of fun. So get out in the backcountry, away from your hectic lifestyle in cities and towns.

Backpacking is a unique, personal experience. It offers many people a rare opportunity to find real freedom and peace away from an often overcrowded and polluted world.

We usually think of backpacking as a leisure activity. But in some places, groups of people travel as a

LEFT

You can see many of the elements of backpacking in this picture — the water, rolling hills, forests, and mountains.

RIGHT

Walking is fun, but sometimes you will just want to take your boots off and relax.

way of life. These **nomads** live a life of packing and unpacking their belongings — and traveling. Usually nomadic people go from one place to another to find food and water for themselves and their animals. The changes of the seasons determine how long the food and water will last in one place, and likewise, how long the nomads will stay. The way nomads deal with their environment can teach backpackers valuable lessons for coping with weather they might encounter on the trail.

L apland lies above the Arctic Circle in the countries of Norway, Sweden, Finland, and part of the Soviet Union. The region is so cold that for seven months of the year, it is covered by snow. Despite the harsh climate, Lapland is home to groups of seminomadic people called Lapps. The River Lapps and the Sea Lapps, with settlements on river banks and sea coasts, generally live

BELOW

The Lapps spend part of each year living in camps set up on the frozen snow.

in log houses. But the Mountain Lapps spend many months each year wandering from place to place.

The Mountain Lapps live in tents pitched on the snow in the wilderness. Some Mountain Lapps herd reindeer, which travel through the mountains in search of vegetation for food. The Lapps follow these reindeer and rely on them for meat, milk, and cheese. Imagine what it must be like living in a tent on frozen snow.

The Lapps are a perfect example of how people can adapt to almost any surrounding, no matter how harsh it seems. Instead of wearing one layer of thick clothing, the Lapps wear many layers of thin clothing. This way they can remove or add layers if they are too hot or too cold. They make simple tents by getting sticks from the forest and covering them with animal skins. They can take these tents down quickly and follow a moving herd of animals. The Lapps also keep their belongings and stored food to a minimum, so that they can pack up quickly and travel fast.

ABOVE

People all around the world use tents to protect themselves from the elements. These tents are used by Himalayan yak herders.

Living in a hot environment is as hard as living in a cold one. The Tuareg live in North Africa's Sahara Desert, a difficult place for any living thing to survive. The nomadic Tuareg travel through the sand dunes and mountains of the desert with their families and animals. They must constantly search for water and food for their livestock. Instead of building permanent homes, the Tuareg set up tents. They push poles of wood deep into the sand and secure them with ropes to keep the strong desert wind from blowing the poles over. Around these ropes, the Tuareg stretch a cover of material to shade themselves from the sun.

The Tuareg carry few belongings, which helps them to pack up their camp quickly and move on. Because they must travel across the hot sand, where water is scarce, the Tuareg must plan carefully before leaving one place for another. If they run out of food and water — or take the wrong route — the results could be fatal.

ABOVE

Tuaregs try to set up camp near a water source, such as an oasis. In the desert, the days are very hot and the nights can be quite cool.

BELOW

The mountains of Nepal present plenty of climatic changes to challenge backpackers.

The nomads, whether in the Arctic Circle or the Sahara Desert, have adapted to their environment. They know the best way to carry their belongings, the best clothes to wear, and the most suitable materials for a tent. Some have discovered how to stay warm in subzero temperatures; others how to stay cool in the heat of the desert. Similarly, backpackers must learn to travel light and stay comfortable, whatever the conditions.

GETTING STARTED

Getting started on a short backpacking or hiking trip is almost as easy as waking up in the morning. Arrange a trip with a small group of friends to start out. Hiking in a group is safer than hiking alone. Once you have practiced map-reading and pathfinding skills, you will have plenty of chances to go out on your own if you want.

In your area, there are probably several other people your age who want to get outside on weekends. Bring some of them together into a group. Maybe your neighborhood or school already has a hiking club. If not, try starting one yourself. Advertise in your school newspaper or put up a few posters. Community groups or youth clubs often offer a range of outdoor activities.

Until you have gained some hiking experience, don't go into unfamiliar territory without taking along an experienced hiker. You can also ask her or him to teach you skills, such as how to read a map and predict the weather.

Before you plan any extended trips, you should gather some basic

RIGHT

When you are first starting, your backpacking trips and hikes will be safer — and probably more fun — if you go with at least one other person.

LEFT

A wilderness camp in the Canadian Rockies

BELOW

There can be a lot of equipment involved in backpacking, and some of it is very expensive. At first you should borrow whatever you can.

equipment. This doesn't mean you have to buy everything. You might be able to borrow or rent what you need. Ask around — you may find people who can lend you a raincoat or a backpack. If you have joined a hiking or backpacking club, the club might have some equipment that members can use or rent. Many outdoors stores rent, as well as sell, much of the equipment you will need.

If you can't borrow what you need, you may be able to buy it secondhand. Look in local outdoors stores and see if they have bulletin boards. People often advertise used camping or hiking equipment on boards like this. A local backpacking or hiking club may also have one. If you aren't sure whether a piece of equipment will work for you, ask a more experienced backpacker.

Another good way to accumulate backpacking equipment is to share the cost with one or more friends. Not everybody can use the equipment at the same time, but you can easily set up a rotation system so that those who share the cost have a scheduled time to use it.

Choosing and fitting boots

Hiking boots come in many different styles and price ranges. When you go to the store, wear your hiking socks and try on as many boots as you can in your price range. With the boot unlaced, you should be able to slide a finger behind the heel. When the boot is laced, you should be able to wiggle your toes, and the boot should be snug around your heel. After you have bought your new boots, break them in on short walks, and gradually increase the amount of time you wear them.

ABOVE

If you have a camera, take it with you on hikes, because you will have many chances to capture stunning photographs.

You can borrow or share most pieces of equipment, but don't share **hiking boots**. Your feet are a different shape and width than your friends' feet, even if they happen to be the same length. After a few outings, a new pair of boots becomes molded to the particular shape of your feet. The more you wear them, the more comfortable they get. If you use someone else's boots, you might get blisters. Try to buy a good pair of new boots from the start.

In the past, most people bought leather boots. Now fabric boots with suede reinforcements are becoming more popular, but they may not last as long. Never go out on the trails in sneakers or running shoes. They are not sturdy enough for most hiking, and they get wet too easily.

One-day hikes are easy to organize because you won't have to sleep outside. This does not mean that you can forget planning altogether, because any hike needs thinking through. How far will you go? What will you do if it rains? Is it likely to be hot? Do you want to take some food with you? How much water will you need? Is there a short route home to take if you find that you have tried to go too far?

For most people, a distance of 10 to 12 miles (about 15 to 20 kilometers) is far enough in a day if they are

Basic equipment checklist
- ✓ Strong boots with a good tread on the soles
- ✓ Waterproof daypack for storing the day's supplies
- ✓ Raincoat, especially a long one that covers much of your legs
- ✓ Water bottle that doesn't leak (If you do not drink water throughout your hike, you could dehydrate.)
- ✓ Orienteering compass
- ✓ Maps
- ✓ Emergency whistle
- ✓ Tarp or bivouac

LEFT

For single-day hikes, a **daypack** should give you enough space for carrying your gear.

> **Waterproof clothing**
>
> *You should always carry a waterproof jacket if you are traveling in a wet climate, or if the weather forecast calls for rain. Waterproof clothing comes in a confusing number of different styles. These are the three main types:*
>
> **1. Waterproof nylon**
> *Keeps you safe from the rain, but traps your body moisture in. If you are working hard, you will become very sweaty.*
>
> **2. Treated breathable nylon**
> *Allows small beads of moisture out, but keeps large drops of water from getting in. This material is quite expensive, but it does not last as long as breathable laminates.*
>
> **3. Inherently breathable laminate**
> *Is waterproof and breathable, but is very expensive.*

let a few drops of rain stop you. There is no real secret to dealing with bad weather—just be prepared and carry a decent waterproof jacket.

The great thing about day hikes is that you do not need to carry much equipment, so you can keep your bag light. If you are hiking with a group, make sure you stick together. When hikers get separated, someone can get lost, and accidents may happen. If you start the day together, finish it the same way. Try to finish your outing before sunset. If you are planning to hike off of established and well-traveled trails, tell people where you will be and how long you plan to be gone. Then, if you happen to get lost or hurt and fail to return, they will know where to begin looking for you. After you have finished your hike, tell the same people that you are done.

If you have been enjoying day-long hikes, you will soon feel the urge to go on overnight trips. Excursions that last a few days must be planned carefully, and they involve a lot of preparation. When you are planning a long trip, figure out where you will sleep each night. Will you camp in a tent or a **bivouac** (a

already used to walking. Check the weather forecast the night before you leave. If bad weather is in the forecast, do not be afraid to change your schedule or plan a different route that keeps you closer to shelter. But don't

makeshift shelter or waterproof bag), or try to find another kind of shelter? Most people find that sleeping in a tent is the best option, because a good tent is the most reliable shelter from rain, snow, and cold wind.

Before you try a camping trip on your own, you should try to get some additional experience by carrying a large pack on the trail for a few days at a time. If you can afford it, one of the best ways to do this without having to buy a lot of camping equipment is to sleep at a **hostel** — a special inn for hikers — along your route.

If you want to sleep out under the stars, the best place to try it at first is as close to home as possible. There are two kinds of bivouacs. One is a makeshift shelter, which can actually be made several ways. To build this kind of bivouac, find a wall or low tree branch and a tarp or a plastic sheet. Drape the tarp so it makes a tent shape, and weigh

ABOVE

Camping with a large group of friends is great fun, especially if there's no one around for you to disturb.

> **Youth hostels**
>
> *In the United States, Canada, and many other countries, there are networks of youth hostels at which you can stay once you have joined a youth hostel association, such as American Youth Hostels. (If you are under 14 you will have to be with an adult.) You have to pay a small amount to stay at a youth hostel.*

BELOW

You can use a tarp to set up a makeshift overnight shelter, or bivouac.

it down with something heavy to keep it from blowing away. The other kind of bivouac is a waterproof bag, also called a **survival bag**, that fits over your sleeping bag to keep it dry in the rain. You can buy one of these bags in an outdoors shop. If you are sure it won't rain, you will probably be more comfortable lying on top of the bag, because it traps body heat inside. If the outside air is cold, you may want to use the bag for extra warmth.

Bivouacs are fine for sleeping outdoors in nice weather, but they are no fun in the rain or snow. If you expect cold or wet weather, you will be more comfortable in a tent — even though you will have to carry extra equipment, such as poles and stakes.

EQUIPMENT

Once you decide to go backpacking overnight, your equipment needs will change considerably. You will need to carry a tent or bivouac, a sleeping bag and mattress, cooking equipment, extra food, and extra clothes. Whether you buy new equipment or borrow most of what you need, there will probably be much more equipment than you have taken with you on your hikes. To carry it all, you will need a good pack, one that is much larger than the small daypack you use for day hikes.

Backpacks with flexible **internal frames** are quickly becoming more popular than backpacks with

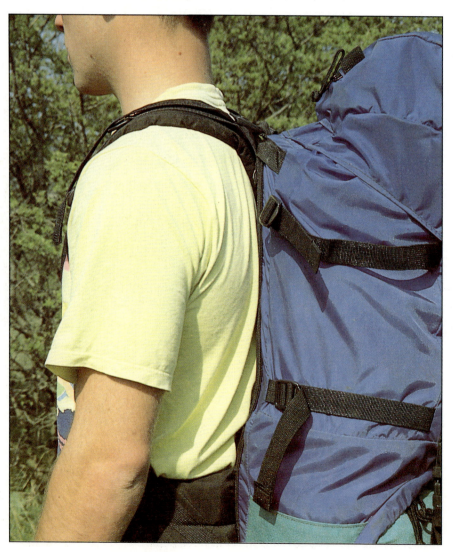

Fitting a backpack
Backpacks come in almost every shape, size, and color. A good backpack will have a well-padded hip belt and well-padded shoulder straps. When you wear the pack, the weight should be on your hips rather than on your back and shoulders. Use one that fits perfectly. Some packs come in fixed lengths and others are adjustable for the distance between your shoulders and hips. If you are still growing, the adjustable kind is best.

LEFT

A correctly fitted backpack

rigid **external frames**. They are usually more comfortable to wear, and they let you maintain good balance on rough terrain.

Backpacks are sized in cubic inches to indicate how much space is available for carrying equipment and supplies. Internal frame backpacks generally range from 3,200 cubic inches to 5,800 cubic inches, but larger and smaller backpacks are available. The best way to get a backpack that feels right is to try on several. If you are buying a new pack, shop in a reputable outdoors store, where the sales staff can help you.

There are two main types of sleeping bag insulation — synthetic and duck or goose down. Synthetic-filled bags are heavier and larger than down bags of the same temperature rating. But they are cheaper, and they will keep you warmer if they get wet. Down bags are expensive and need to be kept perfectly dry at all times, otherwise they will lose their insulating ability.

Sleeping bag ratings

One season .... Summer use
Two season .... Long summer use
Three season .... Spring, summer, and autumn
Four season .... Useable in most conditions
Five season .... Useable in extreme cold

Sleeping bags are rated by season, and by the minimum temperature at which most people can expect to stay warm. A bag that keeps one person warm at 40 degrees Fahrenheit (about 5 degrees Celsius) might not keep someone else warm at the same temperature, but the ratings are a good indication of the type of camping for which the bags can be used.

Most mattresses for camping are made of a closed-cell foam, which does not soak up moisture. These mats are light, cheap, and very effective. Another type of mattress, made of open-cell material, is thicker but can absorb water. Other mats are self-inflating — all you do is unroll them and they fill with air. Usually, though, these types add weight to the pack.

There are many types of **camp stoves**. Before you buy a stove, consider carefully the kind of fuel the stove uses. White gasoline and kerosene stoves can be messy and tricky to use, but the fuel is widely available and inexpensive. Stoves that run off a pressurized canister of fuel (like butane and propane) are easy to use and lightweight. The main drawback of these stoves is that not

BELOW

Tents almost always have two layers — an inner layer that you put up first, and an outer fly that is placed over the top (inset) and tied down.

all canisters fit all stoves, and the canisters are not always reusable.

Tents come in many different shapes. Domed tents give you more head room inside for the floor space than A-frame tents. You will want a tent made of light nylon fabric for backpacking. If you always camp with friends, find a tent big enough for all of you and your equipment, and take turns carrying it on the trail.

Most tents come with a **fly** — a sheet of waterproof material to keep the rain out. The tent wall, then, is made of a breathable fabric that lets out inside moisture and stops condensation. The floor of the tent is usually made of a thicker, more tear-resistant, waterproof nylon.

HIT THE ROAD

During the summer, when the weather is warm, is the best time to start backpacking. Once you have gotten used to the sport, there is nothing to stop you from going during spring and autumn. Winter trips are more difficult and dangerous because of the low temperatures. Even highly experienced backpackers avoid camping in winter, because the weather is usually wet, cold, uncomfortable, and often very unpredictable.

All states have specially reserved **campsites** in state, regional, and national parks. Inside these parks, the land is protected from many kinds of construction projects. These are some of the best areas for backpacking. Before you start out on your trip in a park, find out whether

ABOVE

Once you have set up a camp, you can go out and explore the countryside without loads of equipment.

LEFT

Winter camping is challenging for the experts. Don't try it until you are very experienced.

backpack camping is allowed, and in which areas you will be allowed to set up your camp.

Get a detailed map of the area you pick for a trip. Common **topographic maps** have a **scale** that allows you to see details (1:62,500, 1:50,000, or 1:24,000 are good), and they show hills, rivers, trails, towns, and campsites. The scale of maps is quite simple to understand. On a 1:62,500 map, 1 inch on the map is 62,500 inches (about a mile) on the ground.

Using the map, decide with your group which route to take and how far to go in a day. Remember, when you are backpacking there is no hurry. If you plan your route well, you can take your time and enjoy the scenery and the company. Everyone in the group will have a different level of ability and conditioning. Plan the route at a speed that the slowest person can comfortably manage. There is nothing fun about making people go faster than they want — it will just discourage them from hiking again. Try going 10 miles (16 km) a day. If the ground is rough, you will go more slowly than you would through flat countryside.

When you are gathering your gear for a trip, check it off against a list of things you want to take. Try to be prepared for anything that might happen, but also try to keep your gear to a minimum. If you have to struggle up a hillside with a heavy pack, you won't have a very good time.

As you put things in your backpack, wrap them carefully in plastic bags — especially your sleeping bags and clothes. In a bad storm, rain can find its way into any pack, and wet clothes make backpacking miserable.

Many backpackers have found that it is a good idea to pack everything in a particular order. Once you are out on the trail and you need to find

> **Equipment checklist**
> ✓ Backpack
> ✓ Tent
> ✓ Boots
> ✓ Sleeping bag
> ✓ Camping mattress
> ✓ Stove
> ✓ Fuel bottle
> ✓ Cooking pans
> ✓ Cup, bowl, fork, spoon
> ✓ Water bottle
> ✓ Pocketknife
> ✓ Flashlight
> ✓ Waterproof matches
> ✓ Maps and compass
> ✓ Emergency whistle

BELOW

By the time everything is in it, your backpack will be pretty heavy, so make sure you pack it as comfortably as you can.

something quickly, like a raincoat or pocketknife, it helps to know where in your pack to look. Over the years people have found that if you put the heaviest items close to your back (near the top for established trail hiking, or near the middle for off-trail hiking for the best center of gravity), the pack will be easier to carry. If you

Clothing checklist
✓ Raincoat
✓ Thick sweater
✓ Sweatshirts or shirts (two)
✓ Pants (two pairs)
✓ T-shirts (three)
✓ Thin and thick socks (at least three of each)
✓ Underwear (thermal if possible)

RIGHT

If you are camping overnight, you can use your tent as a base for exploring the area. These people are exploring a city in Nepal.

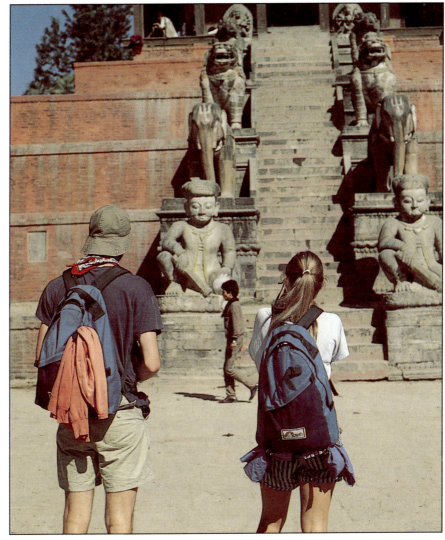

put the heaviest things away from your back, your shoulders will have more weight pulling against them.

Once you have packed everything and completed all your planning, make sure that someone at home knows exactly which route you will take and how long you will be away. Don't leave without writing down these details and leaving them with an adult.

The next step is your first one on the trail. With days of backpacking ahead, you soon start to appreciate the sense of freedom that camping brings. Walk at a steady, even pace to build up your **stamina** and fitness. There is no reason to rush up steep slopes, even if you can. It will only make you hot and tired. Take as many rests as the slowest person in the group wants, but don't hang around too long. As soon as you stop walking, your body starts to cool off quickly. This is when you should put on an extra layer of clothing, quickly!

Wherever you choose to camp, in the backwoods or on a park campsite, you must think carefully about where to put your tent. Most people have trouble sleeping with their feet higher than their heads, so find a site where the ground is fairly flat. Remove any rocks that could poke through the floor of the tent. Also try to picture what will happen if the weather turns rainy. You won't like waking during a storm to find that your spot has turned into a puddle. Avoid the bottoms of slopes, which are bound to become wet in rain.

Whether you are camping in a farmer's field, on a wild mountainside, or at a designated campsite, always take care of the environment.

BELOW

Camping can make an amazing amount of trash. Never leave your trash on the trails or in campsites — always take it away with you. If the site is littered when you get to it, make sure it is cleaner when you leave than it was when you arrived.

BELOW

Maintain a pace that everyone can manage, and stop often for short rests.

Leave the place in exactly the same condition as you found it — or better, if it was in a mess when you arrived. We all produce some trash when we are camping. Carry yours home with you, or put it in a container provided on the site. Never bury trash. It only comes to the surface again, even if it is many years later, and ruins other people's enjoyment.

You should carry a stove instead of relying on camp fires, which are not allowed at some campgrounds. Not only are fires hard on your cooking pots, but sparks can easily cause forest or grass fires.

With each backpacking trip, your knowledge and experience are sure to grow, allowing you to try longer trips, or to trek through more remote areas. Perhaps you will find yourself in another country eventually, where the mountains are higher and the deserts wider than those at home.

HIGH ADVENTURE

With only one day left until we set off at last, after two months of planning, we are actually in the Himalaya Mountains in Nepal. We have food for five days, including the special **dehydrated food** we brought from home. Our boots are waterproofed and the last-minute supply shopping is done. Have we forgotten anything ?

Day 1

It feels great to be out on the trail at last. We were late setting off this morning because we had to wait for a local bus to take us out of town. Walking out of the roadside village and taking the first few steps along the trail was fantastic. The time now is 6 p.m., and it will be dark in half an hour. There is just so much to see, and everything is so different from

LEFT

The passes in the Himalayas are so high that it takes days to walk over them.

ABOVE

On the trail at last! Setting out is always exciting.

what I know at home. The weather is almost tropical here and there are fields of rice on all sides. Of the two weeks of trekking ahead, the next seven or eight days will all be uphill! Today we are on a gentle slope, and my boots feel very comfortable. From the tent door this evening, we can see snow-covered peaks in the distance. We know we will be on the other side of them before long.

Day 2

Last night we camped beside a small stream, about two hours from the last village we had passed. The nights are silent, apart from the buzzing of unseen insects and the gurgling of the stream. I was surprised to find the water in the stream warm this morning. The sun really burns in the middle of the day, but we brought our sunscreen. The path is well used by local people and the surface is muddy from the recent rain. I thought I was quite fit, but my legs were really stiff after the first day of walking. The map shows that we are at an altitude of 6,500 feet (2,000 m). Even after covering 11 miles (about 18 km) today, the mountains ahead still do not look any closer.

Day 4

The Nepalese people have been incredibly friendly. We walked through a small village today, where the houses had thatched roofs and mud walls. We were invited into a house for hot tea. I sometimes turn over in the middle of the night and hear dogs barking in villages miles away. I wonder what the wild animals think of this strange, bright yellow tent. Watching the sun rise over the sharp, rocky ridge to our east is something I will never forget. My backpack is growing lighter — we have eaten most of the food that was in it — and my shoulder muscles feel stronger. However, we need to replace our used-up supplies soon.

RIGHT

If you get a chance to go backpacking in another country, you often find the local people to be very friendly.

Day 6

It was late when we stopped last night — too late really. The whole day had been long and difficult. It was almost dusk as we put the tent up, but thankfully we had found a good camping place before the light faded. We had just enough energy to light our little stove and prepare some hot food. Today is our day off, a rest day after five days of trekking. We were in no great hurry to get out of our warm sleeping bags this morning. The weather is much colder up here. Our bodies are really feeling the effects of the altitude now, so we have to take a day to get used to it. This will *help our bodies cope with the greater altitudes ahead. We are lazing around in the sun on the edge of a pine forest that rises up the steep hillside. Above the hillside, the grassland soon gives out to snow-covered slopes. We have rechecked and packed our equipment for the final push up to the base of the pass tomorrow.*

RIGHT

Part of the fun of a long trek is stopping for a rest in front of a view like this one of the Himalayas.

RIGHT

The view from the top of a pass in the Himalayas shows a whole new world ahead.

Day 7

After one day of rest, my shoulders and legs really ache. I do not know how the Nepalese live up here. Yesterday 10 porters, carrying huge loads of supplies on their backs, overtook us on their way to remote villages uphill. Today the trail is almost straight up, one step above another. I could feel my heel getting sore, and tonight I have a big blister — so much for the tough feet. We are doing well, but now our lungs gasp for more oxygen. It is too cold to sit down now, so when we stop for a rest we just turn and look at the magnificent views that surround us. Today we lunched on dried fruit and chocolate brought from home. The last village is behind us; the land here is too rough and steep for farming. We are alone until we get over the top and down into the next valley.

RIGHT

Stopping to eat in front of dramatic scenery like this is one of the best things about backpacking.

Day 8

We slept badly on this uneven, rocky ground. Crawling from the cozy warmth of a sleeping bag into cold clothes and frozen boots was one of the hardest things I have ever done. We had camped on a rocky ledge that was barely wide enough for the tent. We stopped many times on the way up to drink water from the bottles we had filled at the last stream. At one point, we turned to look back and we could see through the clear air in the distance, the whole valley mapped out beneath us — almost all the route of our last seven days. We reached the top of the pass at about 11:45 a.m., well before the clouds started to build up in the afternoon. Behind us lay the valley we knew, while ahead stretched a whole new world. For 10 minutes we stood there looking at the ridges and unknown mountains that stretched into the distance. It wasn't long before we started to feel cold, so leaving the windswept silence behind, we warmed ourselves with the walk down.

BELOW

Nepalese people often carry heavy loads up the mountain paths.

Day 9

We spent four long hours descending the trail yesterday afternoon. Our knees are now sore from the pounding of 1,000 steps or more. At least it is a few degrees warmer again down here. We spent a lazy morning checking equipment and food supplies. We need to buy some more food again soon. It is a big relief to be over the pass without any problems; now we have five clear days of walking to get back to the road. The land we pass through is always changing. Up here are the ice sheets, where almost nothing lives. As we descend, we will go through every type of habitat. First alpine, then temperate, on into subtropical, and then finally the climate will be tropical once more.

BELOW

If this rickety old bridge had collapsed, the people crossing it would have gotten a very cold bath.

Day 10

The supply of kerosene we brought for our stove is running low. I don't know where we will be able to get any more. I really hate the early morning starts when we fumble with cold, numb fingers at tent poles and stakes. In the last small village we stocked up with supplies — rice, tea, sugar, salt, and eggs. No kerosene.

RIGHT

A shop at the side of the trail can be one of the most welcome sights in the world.

Day 11

I didn't have a chance to finish yesterday's diary entry because, after our visit to the store, we sat in the sun. While we were there, a Nepalese man invited us back to his house for a meal — delicious food and lots of it. Last night we camped on the edge of the village. The people here make the whole trek special. The smell of wood smoke drifts away from each village. Wood is the main source of fuel for cooking and heating. This is, I suppose, how the problems of deforestation start. I am really pleased we brought our own stove and fuel, otherwise we would be making the situation worse. That reminds me, we have to buy more fuel tomorrow, or we'll have big problems.

Day 12

*With each day, I can feel the temperature rising. The main trouble with taking off jackets and heavy pants is that you then have to carry them. We are down to 10,000 feet (3,050 m), and more local people pass us on the way up. They all carry the same load of about 110 pounds (50 kg) each. Up here the valley has a gentle slope, though all that is about to change. The map shows very close **contour lines**, which means a steep descent tomorrow. A landslide has left a scar across the mountain, another product of deforestation. A couple of successes this afternoon brought us fresh milk from a goatherd and kerosene from a small store.*

RIGHT

This woman is carrying a huge load, putting backpackers with their special equipment to shame.

Day 14

I really do not want this trek to end. We spent this, the final day, walking between tropical trees and fields of rice. Children called to us from a village school, and we drank sweet tea in a village tea shop. Porters with empty baskets seem to skip past us with hardly any effort at all. There is no hurry to finish; I would rather we went on for another two weeks. It is really hot, almost too hot down at this level. We drank a quart of water almost every hour to keep ourselves from dehydrating. My boots fit perfectly, apart from the blister, and they give me great traction on any surface. I now trust and understand all the equipment we have. We carried just the right amount, nothing extra and nothing missing. As we neared the end of today's trek, I heard the roar of an engine in the distance; it was a foreign sound I had almost forgotten about. An hour later we found the road and looked back at the white peaks in the distance. We knew then that we would have to return again.

ABOVE

The end of the line — back to civilization, roads, trucks, and noise

TOUGHEN UP

The best way to get in shape for a backpacking trip is to exercise regularly. There are certain muscle areas, such as your leg, shoulder, and back muscles, that require continual toning. Try to develop an exercise program that you can work into your school week without disrupting your studies.

If you take the bus to school, consider leaving early and walking or bicycling instead. Walking will get you in shape for those hikes ahead. Start doing this once or twice a week, and then build up to as many days as you can manage.

Some sports require bursts of energy. For backpacking, the requirements are the opposite. You need a steady flow of energy to keep you going all day. This kind of stored energy is called stamina.

ABOVE AND LEFT

Running and mountain biking both provide good exercise for backpacking, because they strengthen your leg muscles.

In backpacking, the size of your muscles doesn't count as much as your ability to keep going when things get tough. Stamina is important to your safety on the trails, because you won't be tempted to stop so often that the sky turns dark long before you can reach your destination.

When you are planning a fitness routine for a backpacking trip, build up your stamina with exercises that increase your endurance. Bicycling and running — endurance activities — provide good exercise for backpacking. Swimming is the best exercise to prepare your shoulders for carrying a backpack. Carrying a small daypack loaded with books is another good way to get in shape for backpacking. When carrying a pack, always try to keep your shoulders back and your spine straight. Doing this helps your breathing and puts less strain on your back.

WHERE AM I?

Before you go on any kind of backpacking trip, you must be able to use and understand a topographical map and an **orienteering compass**. If you know exactly where you are going, you won't backtrack or make wrong turns. If you do happen to get lost, a map and compass will help you find your way back to familiar territory. Practice your map skills near home before going on the trail alone.

A good map has a lot of details and shows geographical features as symbols. You can translate these symbols into actual landmarks on the ground. Most maps follow a legend that lists what each symbol represents. Topographical maps have

LEFT

The line each of the terraced rice fields follows along this hillside is at the same height, like a contour line on a map.

RIGHT

A topographical map shows you what to expect for terrain in an area. This one is drawn to a scale of 1:24,000.

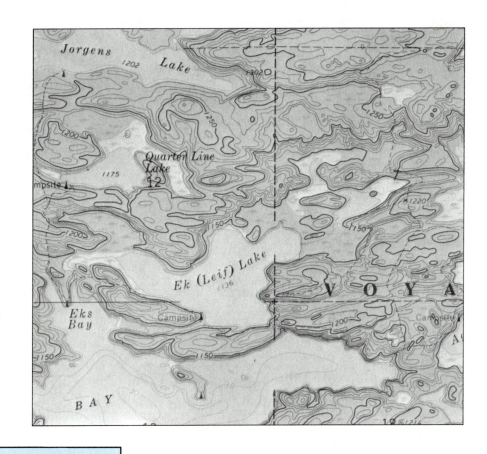

> Compasses point to **magnetic north**, which is different from **true north** (the location of the North Pole) and **grid north** (the north shown on your map). Because of the difference — called **declination** — between magnetic north and the "other" norths, and depending on the location of your hike, you may have to adjust your compass reading. Find a good map and compass book to learn more about adjusting for declination.

contour lines that show the steepness of slopes and indicate the elevation at various points on the slopes.

Topographical maps essentially give you a three-dimensional look at the area you will be hiking. Many contour lines placed close together indicate a steep slope, and a few contour lines spaced far apart show an area that has a gradual slope. When you plot your trek, give yourself more time to hike over terrain that has you walking up and down steep slopes, or plan to cover less ground that day.

Topographical maps also show the locations of lakes, rivers, and forests. You can order maps directly from the U.S. Geological Survey, the primary source for topographical maps of U.S. locations, several months before your trip — or you can get them from a map store.

An orienteering compass makes finding your way around much easier than a standard compass. Without using a map, you can use the compass to get to a landmark you can see in the distance, even if something along the way obscures your view. To read the **bearing**, or direction, point the arrow on the base of the compass toward the landmark.

Getting to some far-off landmark that you can see only on your map is easy with an orienteering compass. Put the compass flat on the map and align an edge of the base along the route you wish to take. Turn the dial of the compass until the parallel lines underneath the needle are parallel to the north-south grid lines on the map. Adjust the compass for declination. Turn the compass around until the needle points toward north on the dial, and walk in the direction indicated by the arrow on the base plate.

Turn the dial on the compass until the needle points north. As long as the needle points toward north, all you have to do is walk in the direction indicated by the arrow on the plastic base of your compass. You will be able to follow this bearing, even if you can no longer see the landmark.

If you can see two landmarks and recognize them on your map as well, you can pinpoint exactly where you are by using your compass and a pencil.

First, read a bearing on one landmark, using the same procedure you would use to hike to a distant landmark.

Hold the bearing (keep the needle on north), and put the compass on the map. Move the map so that one edge of the compass base touches the symbol for the landmark you have chosen, and the lines underneath the needle are parallel to the north-south lines on the map. Use the edge of the compass to draw a line from the landmark.

Repeat this process for a second landmark some distance from your first landmark. You should have two lines on your map that cross. The point at which they intersect is your position.

SURVIVAL SKILLS

Sometimes the best plans go wrong. Someone can get lost, fall, and severely sprain an ankle; or your whole group can get caught in a storm. You will need to know what to do if an emergency arises on the trail. The first thing to remember in all cases is DON'T PANIC. Common sense can help you out of a lot of tricky situations.

If a severe storm has caught you out on the trail, head for the nearest shelter. Once the worst part of the storm has subsided, take the closest safe route back. Keep together and stay on the path.

If somebody has become separated from the main group, stay in one place and use the emergency whistle call: six long whistle blasts, with a minute before the next six. The lost person should answer your call with three whistle blasts. At night, use your flashlight as another signal. Before beginning a search, use a compass to plot your location, and write it down on your map. If it is too dark to see landmarks, establish a base that everyone can find again without having to take bearings. Always leave one person at the base to coordinate the search, and make

ABOVE

If an accident happens in weather like this, you must think clearly and stay calm.

First aid kit contents
+ *Bandages*
+ *Medical tape*
+ *Elastic bandage*
+ *Antibiotic ointment*
+ *Aspirin*
+ *Hydrocortisone cream*

ABOVE

Hiking in groups and taking proper precautions can prevent many accidents.

BELOW

Use your survival bag if you get cold on the trail.

sure that everybody in the search party returns to the base at regular intervals. Work in pairs.

If possible, never leave an injured person alone. If you need to leave for help, put him or her in a sheltered place with a survival bag, plenty of food and water, a flashlight, a whistle, and a raincoat.

You should never keep hiking in the dark unless you are absolutely sure where you are going and the ground is even. If you do get lost in the dark, stay put and protect yourself from the cold by putting on as many layers of clothing as possible. Fill the space around you with twigs and dry leaves, if there are any, to keep more heat next to your body. In an emergency, crawl into a survival bag for more warmth. Do not go to sleep if the temperatures are cold, but concentrate on staying warm. If you get cold, stand up and move around. Loosen your boots and belt to allow your blood to circulate, and eat high-energy food, such as chocolate.

Glossary

Bearing A direction or position, measured in degrees (of a circle, up to 360 degrees), in relation to something else, such as magnetic north

Bivouac A temporary overnight shelter, usually a survival bag or an enclosure made from a tarp

Campsite A place where you pitch a tent. Official campsites frequently have showers that you can use and fire pits where you can cook. If you plan to set up camp away from an official site, check with a ranger first.

Camp stove A small, lightweight stove — usually with a single burner — that burns fuel for cooking food on the trail

Contour lines Brown lines on a map that indicate the height above sea level. The lines can represent 10-foot (3-meter) increases in altitude or other increases, depending on the "contour interval" printed on the map.

Daypack A small backpack, used to carry supplies for a short hike

Declination The difference between magnetic north, which is where your compass points, and either true north or grid north, expressed in degrees

Dehydrated food Food from which water has been removed. You can buy specially packaged dehydrated foods from an outdoors store. On the trail, you can prepare meals by adding water to these foods and heating them.

External frame A type of backpack that has a metal frame to which a cloth pack is attached on the rear side. A hip belt and shoulder straps hold the frame to your body.

Fly A sheet of waterproof material that is placed over a tent to keep rain from getting inside. Tents with these flies are usually made of breathable material that lets small drops of moisture out, preventing condensation.

Grid north The north that appears on a map. Grid north is usually slightly different from true north because mapmakers must distort the true north lines when they transfer their drawings of the round surface of the Earth to a flat piece of paper.

Hiking boots Special boots, made of leather or fabric, that are designed for hiking. These boots give additional support to the parts of the feet that are stressed by hiking. The soles of hiking boots are designed for maximum traction.

Hostel A shelter for hikers, such as a supervised inn for young travelers

Internal frame A type of backpack that has thin metal supports sewn into it to form a frame. The shoulder straps and hip belt are attached directly to the cloth that makes up the pack.

Magnetic north The magnetic field toward which compasses point. Magnetic north is actually over a thousand miles from the North Pole. You will get an accurate compass reading only if you

are standing on the imaginary line that passes through both the North Pole and magnetic north.

Nomads Wanderers who do not have permanent homes, but who travel about in search of food or animals

Orienteering compass A compass that has a base plate with a "direction-of-travel" arrow and a rotating housing that allows you to make adjustments for declination

Scale The comparison between the size of the map and the size of the land that the map represents. On a map drawn to the scale of 1:24,000, 1 unit (such as an inch) on the map equals 24,000 of the same unit on the ground.

Stamina The strength to continue an activity for a long period of time

Survival bag A lightweight, waterproof bag — also called a bivvy bag — that can fit over a sleeping bag to keep it dry. Survival bags can also be used alone, in an emergency, to keep someone warm.

Topographical map A map that shows the surface features, such as hills, trees, rivers, and trails, of an area

True north The north indicated by the North Pole

Books

McVey, Vicki. *The Sierra Club Wayfinding Book.* Boston, Massachusetts: Little Brown, 1989.

Fieldbook. Irving, Texas: Boy Scouts of America, 1984.

Foster, Lynne. *Take a Hike! The Sierra Club Kid's Guide to Hiking and Backpacking.* Boston, Massachusetts: Little Brown, 1991.

Hargrove, Penny, and Noelle Liebrenz. *Backpacker's Sourcebook: A Book of Lists.* Berkley, California: Wilderness Press, 1987.

Jacobson, Cliff. *The Basic Essentials of Map and Compass.* Merrillville, Indiana: ICS Books, 1988.

Randall, Glenn. *The Outward Bound Map and Compass Handbook.* New York, New York: Lyons and Burford, 1989.

Roberts, Harry. *The Basic Essentials of Backpacking.* Merrillville, Indiana: ICS Books, 1989.

Winnett, Thomas. *Backpacking Basics.* Berkley, California: Wilderness Press, 1988.

Video

Backpacking America. Luther, Oklahoma: Harrison and Company, 1986.

More information

American Hiking Society
1015 31st Street N.W.
Washington, D.C. 20007 USA

American Youth Hostels
National Offices
Box 37613
Washington, D.C. 20013 USA

The Sierra Club
730 Polk Street
San Francisco, California 94109 USA

U.S. Geological Survey
Map Sales
Box 25286
Denver, Colorado 80225 USA

Index

American Youth Hostels, 17
Arctic Circle, 6, 9

backpacks, 18–19
bivouac, 15–17, 18
boots, 13

camp stoves, 20–21, 27, 35
clothing, 7, 15, 25, 45
   layering, 7, 45
   types to bring, 25
   waterproof, 15
compass, 40–43, 44
conditioning, 38–39

declination, 41

emergency situations, 44–45

equipment, 12–13, 14, 18–21, 24
   checklist, 14, 24

first aid kit, 44

grid north, 41

hikes, one-day, 14–15
Himalayas, 7, 28–37
hostels, 16, 17

Lapland, 6–7
Lapps, 6–7

magnetic north, 41
mattress, 18, 20

Nepal, 9, 25, 28–37

nomads, 5–9

overnight trips, 15–17, 18–21, 25

planning for trips, 14, 15–17, 23-24, 26

Sahara Desert, 8, 9
sleeping bags, 18, 20
survival bag, 17, 45

tents, 7–8, 15–16, 17, 18, 21, 26
   types, 21
   used in different climates, 7–8
topographical maps, 23, 40–43, 44
true north, 41
Tuareg, 8